to Lady

GILLY and the WHICHAROO

STORY AND PICTURES BY **Glen Dines**

Lothrop, Lee & Shepard Co., Inc. / New York

Copyright © 1968 by Glen Dines · Library of Congress Catalog Card Number: 68-27702 · Printed in the United States of America · All rights reserved

1 2 3 4 5 72 71 70 69 68

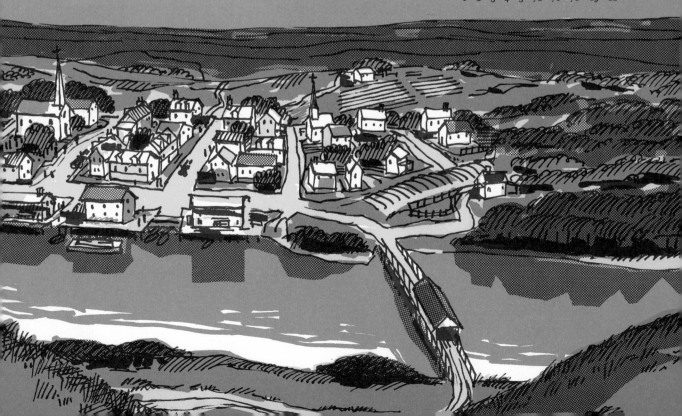

There was once a peaceful little village beside a quiet river. In the village were many skillful goldsmiths. All day long they sat at their work benches quietly making beautiful golden bowls.

The women of the village whispered quietly.

The children played quietly.

Even the dogs of the village barked quietly.

The noisiest thing in the village was the bumpity, battered old goat cart of Gilly Goodwill, the rag boy. All day long Gilly clattered about the streets of the village gathering rags and old pots and pans. The cart squeaked and rattled. The pots and pans jangled and clanked.

"Be quiet!" whispered the fussy Mayor of the village. But no matter how quiet Gilly tried to be, his old cart still squeaked and clattered.

Early one morning the village Lamplighter was tiptoeing about snuffing out the street lamps. Suddenly he saw some huge, strange tracks. "Heavens to Betsy!" the old Lamplighter murmured. He tiptoed to the house of the Mayor. "There are huge, strange tracks in the street," he whispered.

"Gracious sakes alive!" the fussy Mayor murmured. Together they tiptoed to the house of the Sheriff. "There are huge, strange tracks in the street," they whispered.

"Dearie me," the big Sheriff muttered. "I wonder what kind of something or other made these tracks?"

Just then Gilly came clattering down the street. He saw the tracks, too. "That's funny," he said. "Some tracks are deep and some aren't."

"Be quiet!" whispered the fussy Mayor.

"If you ask me," murmured Gilly, "these tracks were made by two something or others—one big and one little."

But no one heard him.

"We'll keep quiet about these tracks," whispered the Mayor. "Perhaps whatever made them will go away."

The others agreed.

That evening the old Lamplighter was tiptoeing about light-
ing street lamps. Suddenly he heard a loud thump-a-bumping
sound. Then he saw the shadow of something huge and strange
on the side of a building. The poor Lamplighter was so frightened he forgot all about being quiet. "Y-I-K-E-S!" he screeched.
He dropped his ladder. He ran as fast as he could.

"A BEAST IN THE STREET!" he shouted. "A BEAST IN
THE STREET!"

The Mayor and the Sheriff and all the villagers came running.

"It was as t-t-tall as a house!" stammered the old Lamplighter. "It made a g-g-great thumping sound when it walked."

Just then Gilly came clattering down the street. "I heard the thumping, too," he said.

"Be quiet!" shouted the fussy Mayor.

"If you ask me," Gilly whispered, "it sounded like a drum." But no one heard him.

"There's a huge, strange beast in our village!" wailed the women. "What are we to do?"

The next morning a horse and coach clip-clopped to a stop before the inn. A tall man stepped out of the fancy coach. Behind him came two servants, one fat and one thin, carrying a big trunk. On the trunk was a fancy sign:

Lord Thornton-Berrybush Beltbuckle the Third
World Famous Catcher of Wild Creatures
and Huge, Strange Beasts

"I have come to your village for some peace and quiet,"
the tall stranger told the Innkeeper.

When the Innkeeper saw the fancy sign on the trunk, he
told the Lamplighter. The Lamplighter told the Sheriff. The
Sheriff told the Mayor. They all hurried to the inn.

"Begging your pardon, your Lordship," the Mayor began,
"but do you catch huge, strange beasts?"

"Indeed I do," answered the stranger.

"Well," said the Mayor, "you have come at a good time.

We just happen to have a huge, strange beast in our village."

"Oh, dear," sighed the stranger. "I've already caught twenty-seven huge, strange beasts this year. I've come to your village for some peace and quiet."

"Would you just look at the huge, strange tracks?" pl[e]
the Mayor.

"Very well," sighed the stranger.

When the stranger saw the tracks, he nodded. "Yes, indeed," he said. "These are huge, strange tracks, all right."

"But what are they the tracks of?" asked the Mayor.

"These are the tracks of a middle-size, multicolored, River Water Whicharoo," answered the stranger. "I've caught many of them—but never this far north."

"Would you please catch this one?" the villagers begged.

"Oh, very well," sighed the stranger. "But only if you help me. Perhaps then I can get some peace and quiet."

"We'll help you!" shouted the villagers.

"First," said the stranger, "we'll make secret signs on the walls for the Whicharoo to see.

"Then," said the stranger, "we'll hang bells and rattles on the trees for the Whicharoo to hear.

"Finally," the stranger announced, "we must build a trap large enough to catch a middle-size Whicharoo."

It was late afternoon before the trap was completed.

"Secret signs and bells and rattles are good," said the stranger. "But there's one sure way to get the Whicharoo into the trap. Whicharoos love to swallow shiny things—especially shiny, *golden* things," the stranger added, wiggling his eyebrows. "If only we could leave a trail of shiny, *golden* things from the river to the trap."

"We'll use our golden bowls," shouted the goldsmiths.

"Yes, indeed," the stranger agreed, rubbing his hands.

"But what happens to the golden bowls the Whicharoo

swallows?" asked Gilly before the fussy Mayor could tell him to be quiet.

"Nothing at all, you silly little boy!" the stranger snapped. "Once we catch the Whicharoo, we will tickle it until it coughs up all the golden bowls it swallowed."

"Yes! Yes!" shouted the goldsmiths. "We'll tickle the Whicharoo!"

"But wouldn't old pots and pans do as well?" asked Gilly.

"Go away, you silly little boy!" said the stranger.

"And take your noisy goat cart," shouted the goldsmiths.

Away clattered Gilly with his bumpity, battered old goat cart. He decided to look for rags behind the village inn. He found the stranger's horse and coach instead.

"If only I had a fancy coach like that," Gilly sighed. "I could ride about the village as quietly as can be."

Just then the fat servant and the thin servant came hurry-

ing out of the inn carrying the stranger's big trunk. They loaded the trunk into the coach. Out of the trunk they took a drum and four huge, strange things for making Whicharoo tracks.

The two servants scurried down the street toward the river. Gilly scampered up the street as fast as he could go.

"Mr. Mayor!" Gilly shouted. "Mr. Mayor!"

"Be quiet!" ordered the fussy Mayor. "Can't you see I'm busy?"

"But I saw the two servants," Gilly whispered. "They had a drum and four things for making Whicharoo tracks."

Of course, no one heard him.

Meanwhile, the stranger stood at the other end of the street. "Whicharoos are too horrible to look at!" he shouted. "All women and children must get inside. Close the shutters. Bar the doors. All men in the street must hide and cover their eyes. Like this!" he ordered, tying a large handkerchief over his own eyes.

"Has everyone covered his eyes?" he asked.

"Yes, yes," answered the men.

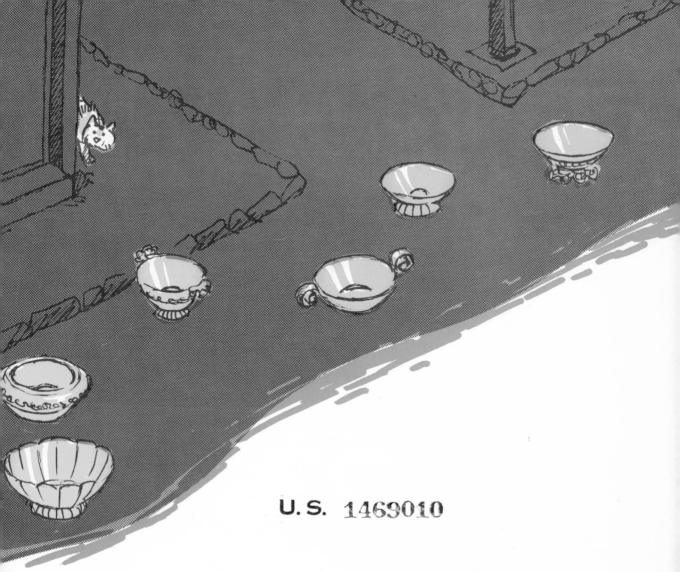

Now, as soon as the stranger knew no one was looking, he took off his blindfold and waved his arms. A loud thump-a-bumping sound echoed in the street.

"The Whicharoo is coming!" warned the stranger.

But it wasn't a Whicharoo at all. It was the fat servant making Whicharoo sounds with the drum.

Scurrying beside him was the thin servant scooping the golden bowls into a sack.

"Thump Bump," thundered the drum as the fat servant waddled up the street making deep Whicharoo tracks.

"The Whicharoo is closer!" warned the tall stranger.

"Thump Bump!" thundered the drum as the skinny servant scuttled up the street making not-so-deep Whicharoo tracks.

"The Whicharoo is here!" shouted the stranger as he and the two servants climbed into the coach.

At that very moment, something huge and strange *did* come bumping and thumping up the street . . .

. . . lurching and bouncing . . . clanging and banging.

"IT *IS* A WHICHAROO!" screeched the stranger. He and the servants were so frightened they tumbled backwards in the coach. The horse was so frightened it galloped away, pulling the coach up the street . . .

. . . straight into the big trap.

KAA-LUMP went the trap door.

KAA-RASH went the coach on its side, wheels spinning.

KAA-LATTER went the golden bowls, tumbling out of the sack.

"Hooray!" shouted the men, hearing the uproar. "We've caught the Whicharoo!"

The women and children came running into the street. "But where is it?" they asked.

"In the trap!" answered the men as they took off their blindfolds.

"Looks more like a horse and coach!" cried the women.

"And a drum!" exclaimed the children. "With things for making Whicharoo tracks!"

"And all our golden bowls!" shouted the goldsmiths.

"The three sneaky thieves!" muttered the big Sheriff.

"Then *that* must be the Whicharoo!" shouted the Mayor when he saw the huge, strange shape rumbling toward them.

"YIKES!" screeched the Lamplighter. "Run for your lives!"

"Wait," came a voice from inside the clattering heap. "It's me." And out from under the great pile of rags and old pots and pans stepped Gilly Goodwill. "I only wanted to frighten the stranger," he explained.

"Hooray for Gilly!" the goldsmiths cheered. "He trapped the stranger and saved our golden bowls."

"We must give him a reward," said the Mayor. "Gilly, what would you like most of all?"

Gilly whispered his answer, and for once the Mayor listened to every word.

"A well deserved reward indeed," the Mayor announced.

The stranger and his servants were locked in jail. The big trap was taken apart. The bells and rattles and secret signs were taken down. Soon the village was as quiet as before . . .

. . . even quieter. Gilly never again clattered about in an old bumpity, battered goat cart. Instead he clip-clopped quietly in his well deserved reward—the stranger's fancy coach. Together with Gilly and his goat went the children and sometimes even the fussy Mayor of the peaceful little village beside the quiet river.